11/20

P9-DCA-241

Lebanon Public Library
104 E. Washington St.
Lebanon, In 46052

Ten in the Bed

for Felice
—J.C.

Text and Illustrations © Jane Cabrera 2006
First published in Great Britain in 2006 by Gullane Children's Books.
First published in the United States of America in 2006 by Holiday House.
All Rights Reserved
HOLIDAY HOUSE is registered in the U.S. Patent and Trademark Office.
Printed and bound in February 2020 at Toppan Leefung, DongGuan City, China.
www.holidayhouse.com
This Jane Cabrera's Story Time edition first published
in 2020 by Holiday House Publishing, Inc.
1 3 5 7 9 10 8 6 4 2

The Library of Congress has cataloged the prior edition as follows:

Library of Congress Cataloging-in-Publication Data

Cabrera, Jane.
Ten in the bed / by Jane Cabrera. — 1st ed.
p. cm.
Summary: In this version of the traditional nursery rhyme, each of the sleepers who fall, leap, bounce,
or wobble out of bed when the little one says "move over" represents a different profession.
ISBN-13: 978-0-8234-2027-8 (hardcover)
ISBN-10: 0-8234-2027-8 (hardcover)
1. Nursery rhymes. [1. Nursery rhymes. 2. Occupations—Fiction. 3. Counting. 4. Stories in rhyme.]
I. Title: Ten in the bed. II. Title.
PZ8.3.C122A15 2006
[E]—dc22
2005035880

ISBN: 978-8-8234-4482-3 (hardcover)

Ten in the Bed

Jane Cabrera

HOLIDAY HOUSE NEW YORK

Here is the **Little One,**
A tired and sleepy head.
Stretching and yawning,
He's ready for bed.

But . . .

10

There were **ten** in the bed
And the **Little One** said,
"Move over, move over."

So they all rolled over
And the **snorer**
fell out.

So they all rushed over
And the **Cook fell out.**

There were **eight** in the bed
And the **Little One** said,
"Move over, move over."

So they all bounced over
And the **Trumpeter fell out.**

7

There were **SEVEN** in the bed
And the **Little One** said,
"Move over, move over."

So they all groaned over
And the DOCTOR
fell out.

There were **Six** in the bed
And the **Little One** said,
"Move over, move over."

So they all leaped over
And the **Ballerina fell out.**

There were **five** in the bed
And the **Little One** said,
"Move over, move over."

So they all swayed over
And the **Pirate fell out.**

4

There were **four** in the bed
And the **Little One** said,
"Move over, move over."

So they all bowed over
And the **Princess fell out.**

There were
three in the bed
And the **Little One** said,
"Move over, move over."

So they all wobbled over
And the **Pilot**
fell out.

3

2

There were **two** in the bed
And the **Little One** said,
"Move over, move over."
So the Astronaut floated over
And **she fell out.**

There was **one** in the bed
And **everyone** said,
"Move over, move over."

So the Little One moved over
And he . . .

Snorer

Cook

Trumpeter

Doctor

Ballerina

. . . they all danced about!
Then the Little One screamed
And he gave a big shout . . .

"Settle down now,
settle down now!"

So they all settled down and went to sleep.
There was not a sound, there was not a peep.
Until the Little one said . . .

"Good night!"